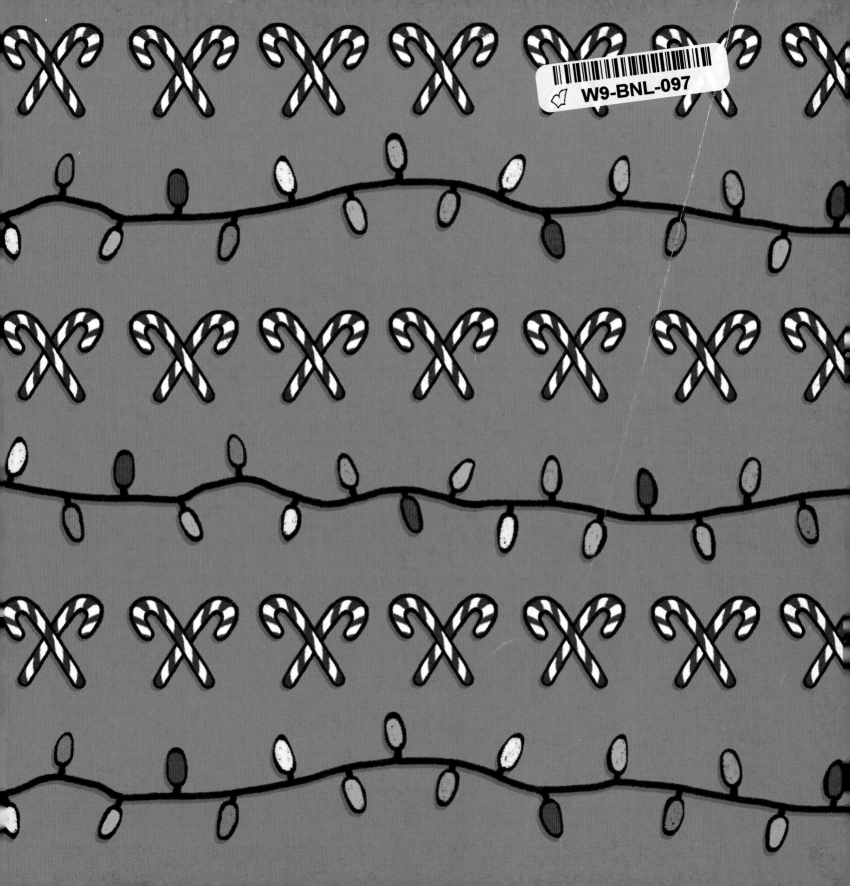

In memory of
Debbie Alvarez

First published in the United States of America in September 2016
by Bloomsbury Children's Books
www.bloomsbury.com

Bloomsbury is a registered trademark of Bloomsbury Publishing Plc

For information about permission to reproduce selections from this book, write to
Permissions, Bloomsbury Children's Books, 1385 Broadway, New York, New York 10018
Bloomsbury books may be purchased for business or promotional use. For information on bulk purchases please
contact Macmillan Corporate and Premium Sales Department at specialmarkets@macmillan.com

Library of Congress Cataloging-in-Publication Data
available upon request
ISBN 978-1-68119-155-3 (hardcover)
ISBN 978-1-68119-156-0 (e-book) • ISBN 978-1-68119-157-7 (e-PDF)

Art created digitally using Adobe Photoshop
Typeset in Maiandra
Book design by Colleen Andrews
Printed in China by Leo Paper Products, Heshan, Guangdong
1 3 5 7 9 10 8 6 4 2

All papers used by Bloomsbury Publishing, Inc., are natural, recyclable products
made from wood grown in well-managed forests. The manufacturing processes
conform to the environmental regulations of the country of origin.

Penguin's Christmas Wish

Salina Yoon

BLOOMSBURY

NEW YORK LONDON OXFORD NEW DELHI SYDNEY

It was Christmas Eve. Pumpkin was getting ready for the best holiday ever. "I wish we had a real Christmas tree." Pumpkin sighed.

Penguin knew there were no pine trees on the ice. But he had an idea.

Penguin packed the sled for a long journey.

Bootsy carried the ornaments,

Pumpkin held the star,

and Grandpa took the presents.

Penguin led them away from their frozen home.

Deep in the heart of the forest,
a special friend was waiting.

Pinecone! My,
how you've grown!

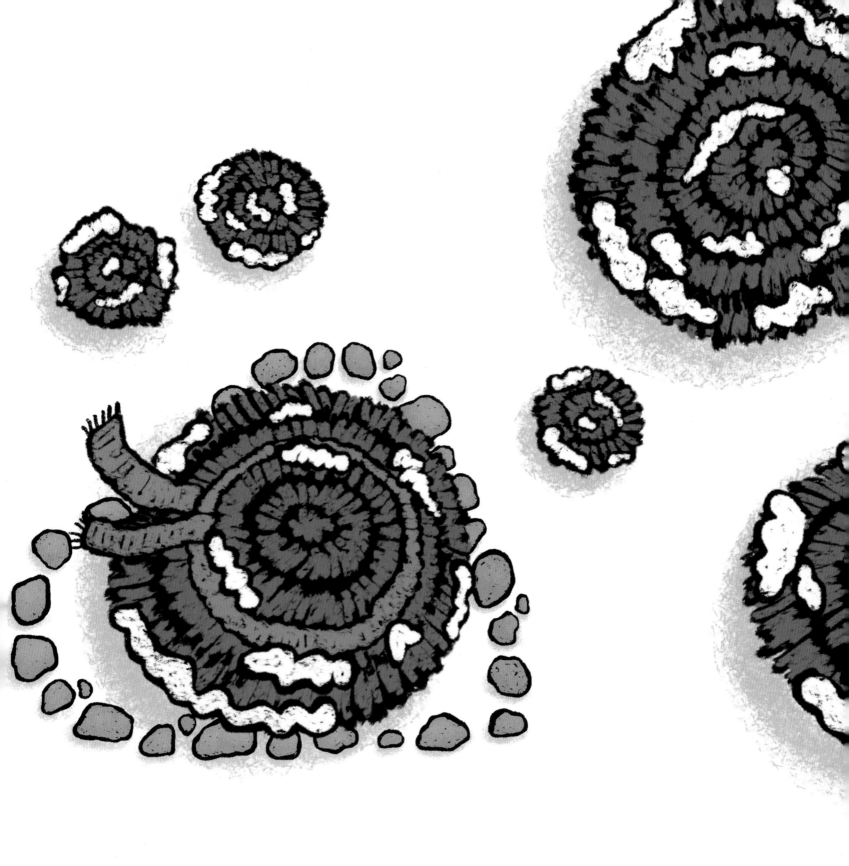

The penguins
decorated Pinecone
with all the trimmings.

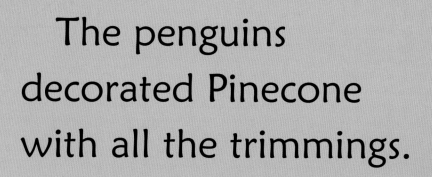

Now we're ready
for Christmas!

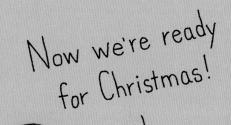

"What a fine tree," said Grandpa.

That night, the penguins
dreamed of Christmas wishes.

Penguin wanted to share Christmas with the whole forest. But there wasn't anyone else around.

While the penguins slept, a
blizzard swept through the forest.
The wind blew and blew.

On Christmas morning, the penguins returned. Not a single decoration hung from the tree.

And all the presents were gone.

The star is missing!

"Christmas is not about decorations and presents," said Grandpa. "It is about being with the ones you love."

Penguin set off into the snow.

Penguin searched high and low. All
he could find were branches and twigs.

They were exactly
what he needed . . .

. . . for the perfect presents for everyone.

Knitting needles! Just what I wanted!

Drumsticks! I can't wait to play with them!

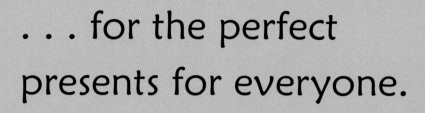

The penguins had a lovely day.

Grandpa and Penguin
caught Christmas dinner.

Bootsy knit a
trunk cozy.

Rum-pa
pum-pum!

Pumpkin drummed
Christmas carols.

Everyone's Christmas
wish had come true . . .

. . . except for Penguin's.

Just then, the sun
warmed the air, and
the snow began to melt.

By nightfall, Penguin
noticed something.

Look!

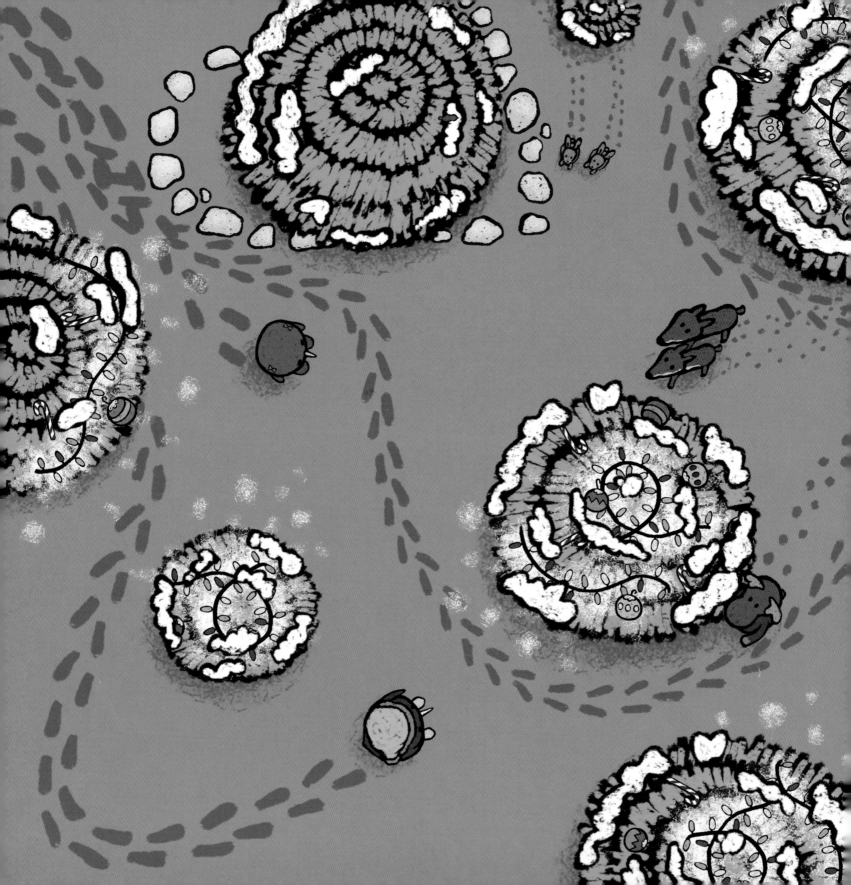

The storm had blown Pinecone's decorations onto every tree. And the magic of Christmas lit up the forest!

Friends both old and new
gathered from far and wide.
Penguin's Christmas wish had
come true!

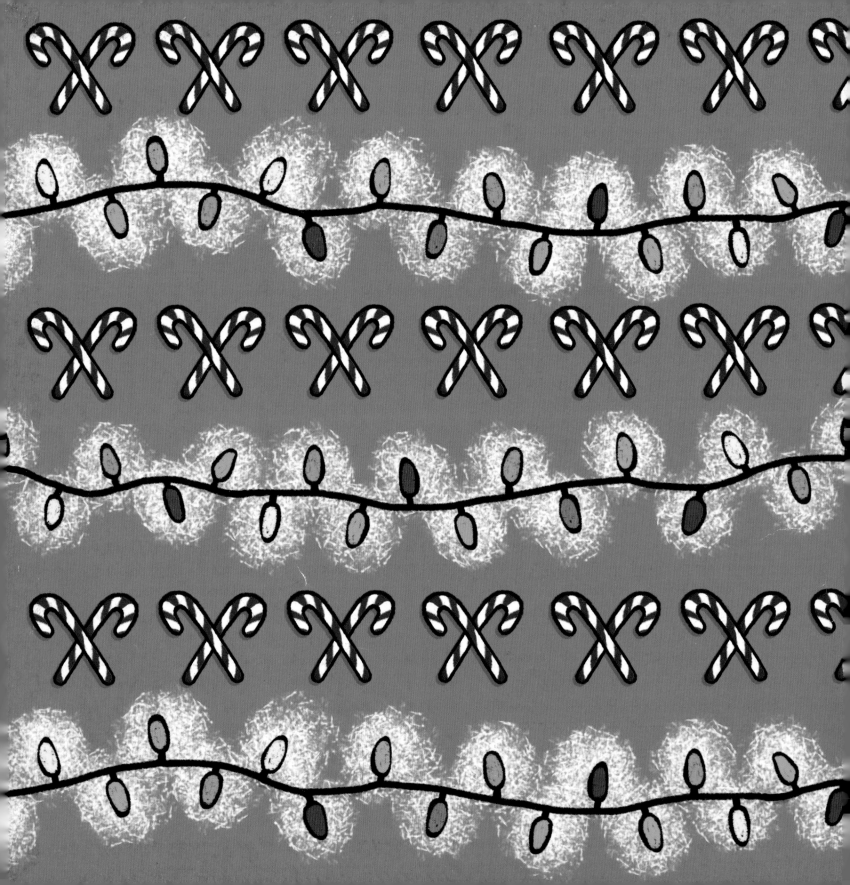